Dear Parents:

Congratulations! Your child is taking the first steps on an exciting journey. The destination? Independent reading!

STEP INTO READING® will help your child get there. The program offers five steps to reading success. Each step includes fun stories and colorful art or photographs. In addition to original fiction and books with favorite characters, there are Step into Reading Non-Fiction Readers, Phonics Readers and Boxed Sets, Sticker Readers, and Comic Readers—a complete literacy program with something to interest every child.

Learning to Read, Step by Step!

Ready to Read **Preschool–Kindergarten**
• big type and easy words • rhyme and rhythm • picture clues
For children who know the alphabet and are eager to begin reading.

Reading with Help **Preschool–Grade 1**
• basic vocabulary • short sentences • simple stories
For children who recognize familiar words and sound out new words with help.

Reading on Your Own **Grades 1–3**
• engaging characters • easy-to-follow plots • popular topics
For children who are ready to read on their own.

Reading Paragraphs **Grades 2–3**
• challenging vocabulary • short paragraphs • exciting stories
For newly independent readers who read simple sentences with confidence.

Ready for Chapters **Grades 2–4**
• chapters • longer paragraphs • full-color art
For children who want to take the plunge into chapter books but still like colorful pictures.

STEP INTO READING® is designed to give every child a successful reading experience. The grade levels are only guides; children will progress through the steps at their own speed, developing confidence in their reading.

Remember, a lifetime love of reading starts with a single step!

Licensed by Hasbro. Published in the United States by Random House Children's Books, a division of Penguin Random House LLC, 1745 Broadway, New York, NY 10019, and in Canada by Penguin Random House Canada Limited, Toronto, in conjunction with Disney Enterprises, Inc.

Visit us on the Web!
StepIntoReading.com
rhcbooks.com

Educators and librarians, for a variety of teaching tools, visit us at RHTeachersLibrarians.com

ISBN 978-0-593-17300-8 (trade)
ISBN 978-0-593-17301-5 (lib. bdg.)
ISBN 978-0-593-17302-2 (ebook)

Printed in the United States of America
10 9 8 7 6 5 4 3 2 1

STEP 3 STEP INTO READING®
READING ON YOUR OWN

LOST BOTS!

by Lauren Clauss

illustrated by Hasbro

Random House New York

Some time ago, at a mall just like any other, an odd mist suddenly appeared.

The mist was full of Energon,
a special Transformers energy
that turned objects into . . .

Transformers BotBots!
Hidden in plain sight, the BotBots
liked to explore the mall
they soon called home.

The BotBots formed tribes
based on the stores they came from.
Each tribe has its own customs,
values, and rules.

But one tribe is different
from all the others.
The *Lost Bots* came to life
in the mall's Lost and Found.

They are from different tribes,
but they now live together
in peace.

One day, the *Lost Bots* Dimlit
and Stinkeye Stapleton are playing.
They see S'up Dawg and Hawt Diggity
from the *Greaser Gang*.
Those bots appear
to have a lot in common,
and Dimlit wonders why he is not
in a tribe with bots who are
more like him.

Dimlit gathers a group of *Lost Bots* who feel the same way. They decide to search the mall to find the tribes each of them came from.

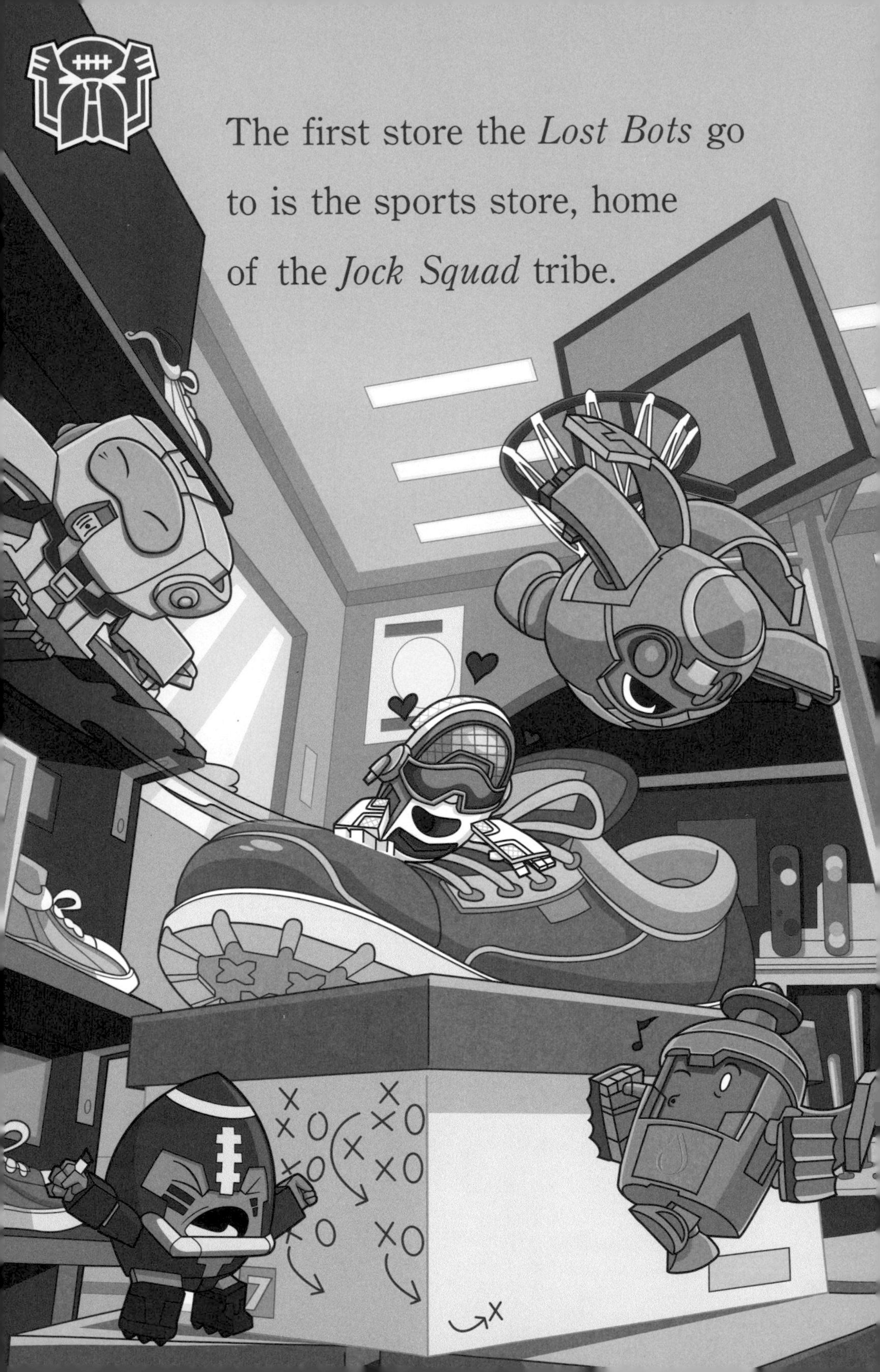

The first store the *Lost Bots* go to is the sports store, home of the *Jock Squad* tribe.

Lovestruck and Kikmee see other balls.
They think it is where they belong!
But Toughdown, a football bot,
tackles them! They run away.
The other *Lost Bots* don't play so rough!

Next, the *Lost Bots* see
the signs at the health-food store.
It is home to the *Fresh Squeezes*!

Greeny Rex thinks they will like her magical healing herbs. Greeny gets some greens to share with the tribe. But she is scared by the battle-ready Sensei Spiney, who just wants to fight!

Greeny realizes that the *Fresh Squeezes* might not be good for her health!

The *Lost Bots* enter Sprinkles,
the sweets shop and home
of the *Sugar Shocks* tribe.
With a name like Sprinkles,
Sprinkleberry Duh'Ball and Frostferatu
must belong here!

But Frostferatu scares the *Shocks*

when he tries to bite

the Plop Father's cannoli filling.

Sprinkleberry Duh'Ball watches

as Plop Father runs off screaming.

They know they're too tart

for these treats now!

Trisourtops follows a stinky smell to the home of the *Spoiled Rottens*.

He's sure that he belongs with
the smelliest tribe in the mall!
When Trisourtops meets Moldwich,
the rottenest of the bunch,
neither one of them likes
what they smell.
Trisourtops quickly leaves.
Being a *Spoiled Rotten* stinks!

Stinkeye Stapleton notices
a very organized store. He goes to see
which tribe keeps such a neat home.
It is the *Backpack Bunch*!

But Stinkeye Stapleton's no-mess
attitude scares Ms. Take.
If there weren't any mistakes
to erase, she wouldn't have a job!
She runs away.
Stinkeye feels bad
and leaves the store.

Smooth Shaker breaks off from the group when he sees a store with musical instruments. He feels some seriously good vibes in there!

He meets the *Music Mob*.
Soon Pink Key Pop and Batterhead
start rocking out.
Smooth Shaker learns that this tribe
is too heavy-metal for his smooth jams.

The Detangler always wants to keep things neat. He heads for the bathroom, home of the *Toilet Troop*. He thinks that is where he can help the most!

After seeing Stinkosaurous Rex
use Nobeeho as deodorant,
Detangler can't even imagine
what the *Troop* would do with him!
He flushes his dreams of joining them
right down the drain.

The colorful windows at the home of the *Swag Stylers* catches Fail Polish's eye.

She runs into the fashion store,
leaving a pink trail behind her.
Fail Polish bumps into Chic Cheeks.
Chic takes one look at the pink mess
and makes her leave.

That's fine with Fail Polish.
The *Swag Stylers* clash
with her style anyway.

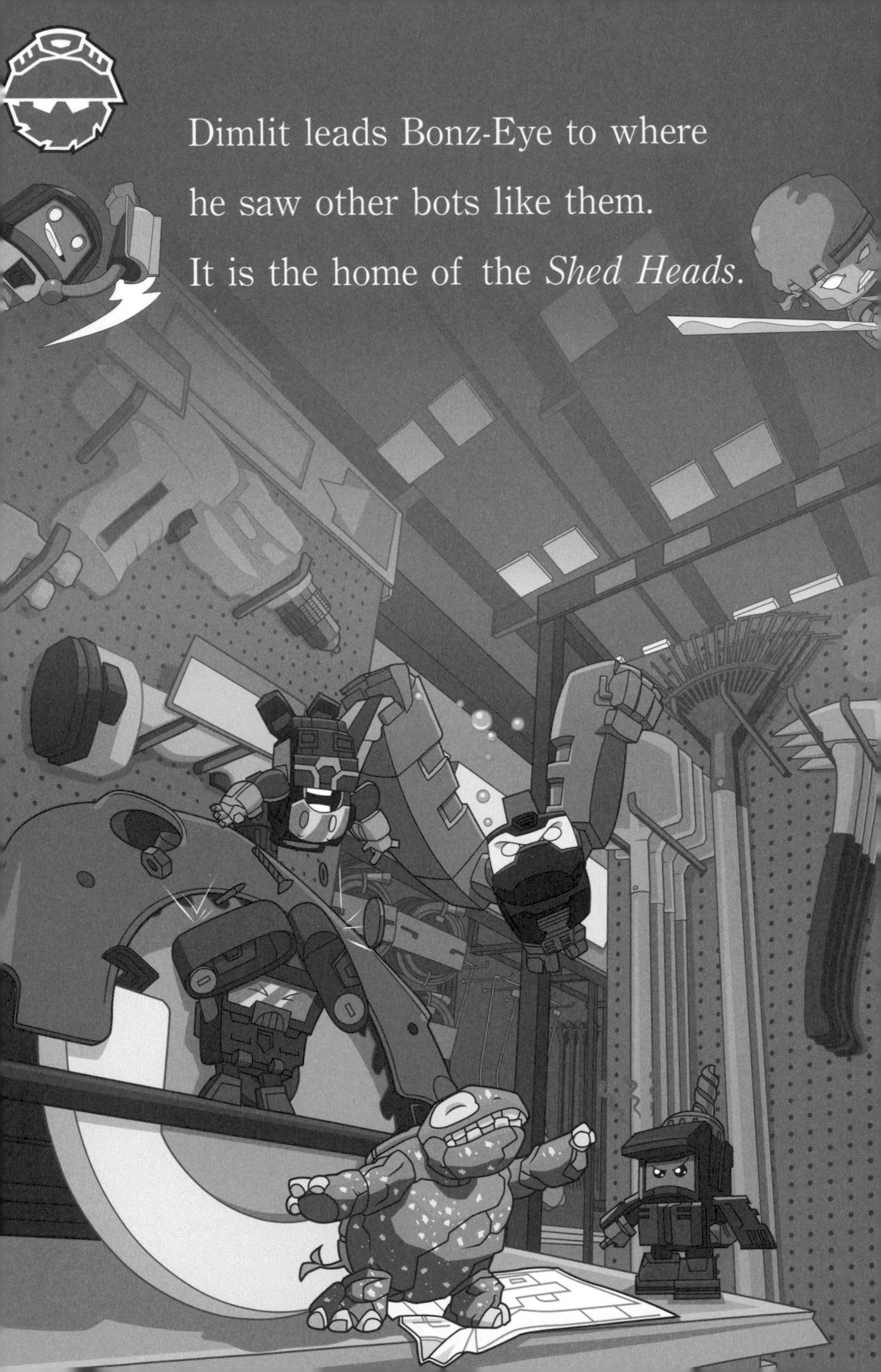

Dimlit leads Bonz-Eye to where he saw other bots like them. It is the home of the *Shed Heads*.

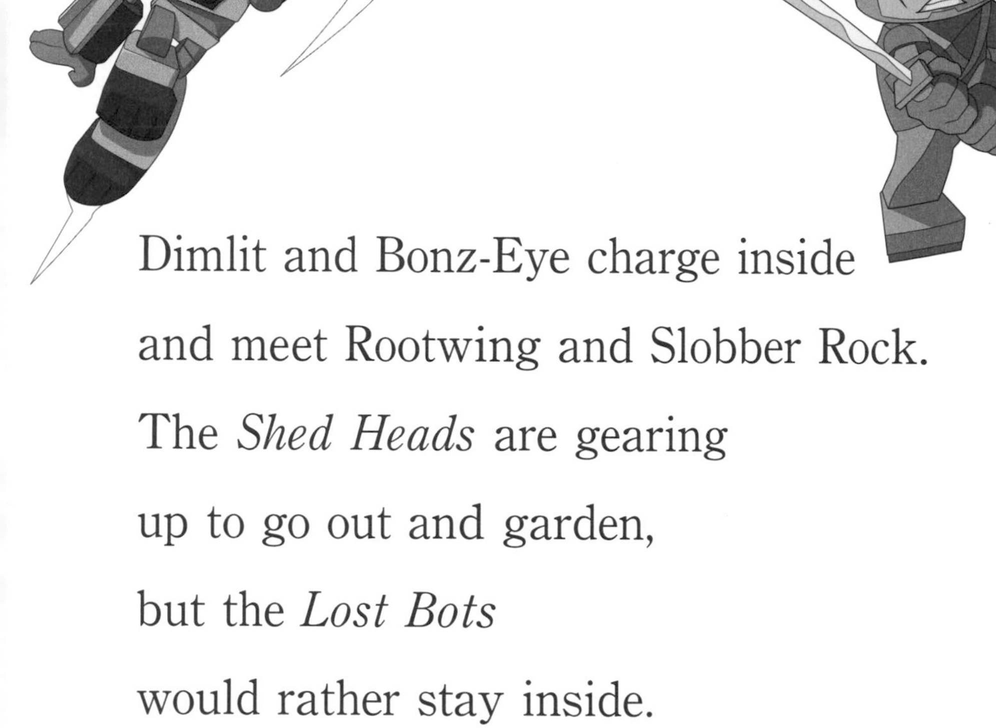

Dimlit and Bonz-Eye charge inside
and meet Rootwing and Slobber Rock.
The *Shed Heads* are gearing
up to go out and garden,
but the *Lost Bots*
would rather stay inside.
They are indoor bots!

Dimlit feels bad about leading the other *Lost Bots* on the search. No one found the right tribe for themselves.

But as Dimlit walks back
to the Lost and Found,
he sees his *Lost Bot* friends
laughing and playing.
They are happy
together!

Dimlit and the other *Lost Bots* realize they have always been right where they belong. They get ready for their next wild adventure. Who knows what they will find!